Usborne
Ballet
Stories
for Bedtime

Retold by Susanna Davidson and Katie Daynes

Illustrated by Alida Massari

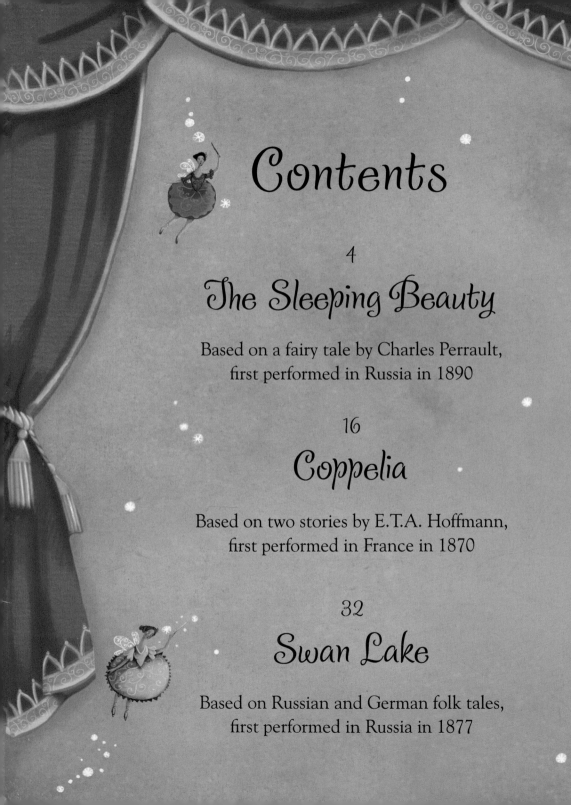

Contents

4

The Sleeping Beauty

Based on a fairy tale by Charles Perrault,
first performed in Russia in 1890

16

Coppelia

Based on two stories by E.T.A. Hoffmann,
first performed in France in 1870

32

Swan Lake

Based on Russian and German folk tales,
first performed in Russia in 1877

48

La Sylphide

Based on a story by Charles Nodier,
first performed in France in 1832

60

Don Quixote

Based on a novel by Miguel de Cervantes,
first performed in Russia in 1869

72

The Nutcracker

Based on a story by E.T.A. Hoffmann,
first performed in Russia in 1892

84

La Fille Mal Gardée

Inspired by a painting by Pierre-Antoine Baudouin,
first performed in France in 1789

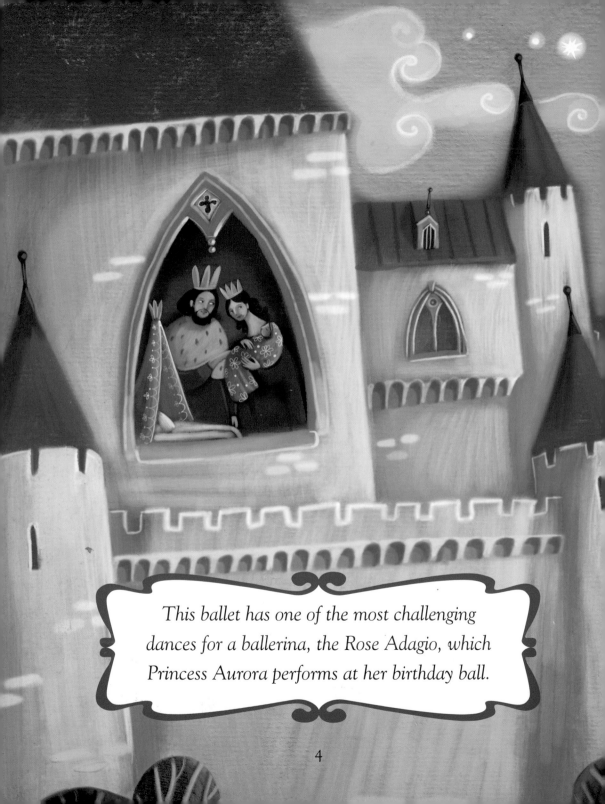

This ballet has one of the most challenging
dances for a ballerina, the Rose Adagio, which
Princess Aurora performs at her birthday ball.

The Sleeping Beauty

Far away and long ago, a queen gave
birth to a beautiful baby princess.
"Let's call her Aurora," her
parents decided.

The king wanted a huge celebration. He invited everyone he could think of to the christening. Soon the castle was alive with music and laughter and dancing.

Fairies from across the kingdom were asked to be godmothers to the baby princess. They blessed her with their gifts.

I give you beauty...
intelligence...
a sweet temper...
grace...
you shall sing like
a nightingale...
and dance like an angel...

The fairies spun around the cradle, sprinkling magic dust

with their wands, until only the Lilac Fairy had her gift left to give.

But before she could speak there was a clap of thunder followed by a stream of smoke, which snaked its way through the castle. Out of the smoke came Carabosse, the evil fairy, in a carriage drawn by scampering, prancing red-eyed rats. She swept up to the king and queen.

"So you're having a party!" she snarled. "Why didn't you invite me?"

"I f-f-forgot..." stammered the king.

"Well you'll pay for that," cackled Carabosse. She peered into the cradle. "I'll give you a gift, princess," she hissed. "On your sixteenth birthday, you will prick your finger and die!" Carabosse cackled once more, then, with a thunderclap, she vanished from the castle.

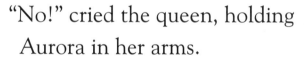

"No!" cried the queen, holding Aurora in her arms.

"I still have my gift," said the Lilac Fairy, fluttering towards them. "I can't lift the curse, but I can weaken it. Aurora won't die; she will fall into a deep sleep – a sleep that can only be broken by a kiss from a prince."

"Thank you," sobbed the queen, while the king strode through the castle, banning all sharp objects from his kingdom.

The years passed and Princess Aurora grew up to be everything her fairy godmothers had wished for – she was beautiful and graceful, clever and kind.

On her sixteenth birthday, the king and queen held a glittering ball. Princes from across the land tried to win her heart. All Aurora wanted to do was dance.

As she twirled away from her suitors, an old woman slipped a bouquet of roses into her hands. "I brought these specially for you, my dear," she said.

"Thank you," replied Aurora, lifting the roses into the air.

She tightened her grip and felt a sharp prick... a drop of blood formed on her fingertip and then she dropped, lifeless, to the ground.

With a triumphant laugh, the old woman flung off her cloak. "It is I, Carabosse!" she cried, then fled the castle grounds.

The king and queen rushed over to Aurora, but there was nothing they could do.

"Remember," the Lilac Fairy comforted them, "she is not dead, only sleeping."

She waved her wand, casting a spell of slumber over the castle. Maids serving, jesters joking, jugglers juggling – everyone fell asleep in an instant. Creepers and vines clambered over the castle walls, hiding it from view.

A hundred years passed. The castle was silent and still, except for the leaves on the castle walls, rustling in the wind.

Far away to the east, a prince was riding through a forest, his royal friends beside him as they hunted a stag.

But the prince hung back, letting his friends go on. He felt nervous, excited... as if something were about to happen; something that would change his life forever.

As soon as he was alone, the Lilac Fairy appeared before him. "Let me show you a vision," she whispered.

The prince looked up to see Princess Aurora shimmering in the air. "Who is she? Where is she?" asked the prince, reaching out for her.

"Follow me," replied the Lilac Fairy.

She led him across a silver lake and pointed to a distant turret. "Her name is Princess Aurora and she lies sleeping there," she told him. "Only you can rescue her."

The prince rode hard and fast to the castle, then fought his way through the tangled forest, thrashing aside thorns and brambles. At last, with a beating heart, he reached the castle gates.

"Stop!" cried a voice. "I will not let you enter."

The prince turned to see Carabosse, her claw-like hands outstretched as she forced the prince back with her magic.

"You can't stop me," said the prince, thinking only of Aurora as he burst through the castle gates.

Inside, he climbed a turret, his feet echoing on the cold stone stairs.

There, in the topmost tower, lay Princess Aurora. The prince knelt down... and kissed her.

Aurora woke and gazed up at the prince. "Have you come at last?" she said.

The prince nodded. "Marry me?" he asked, sweeping her up in his arms.

The creepers and vines melted away and the castle was filled with life once more. Aurora and the prince rushed to tell the king and queen,

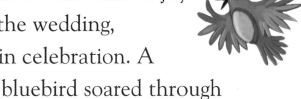

who heard their news with tears of joy.

On the day of the wedding, everyone danced in celebration. A bluebird soared through the air and fairytale characters came to join the party. Puss in Boots sprang through the hall, while Little Red Riding Hood darted between the guests, followed by a wolf flashing his teeth in a wicked smile.

Then the prince and Aurora took to the floor in a swirling, dreamlike dance. Hovering overhead, the Lilac Fairy held high her wand and smiled. Here, at last, was a happy ending for them all.

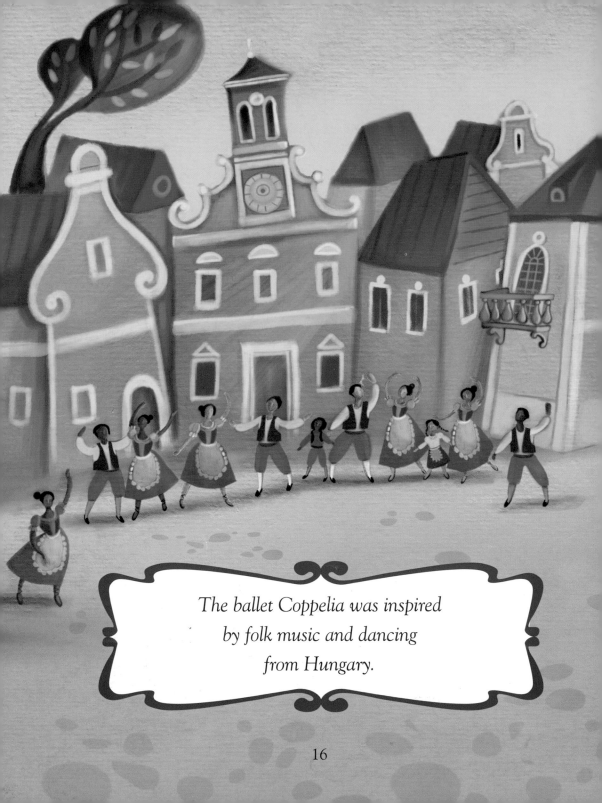

The ballet Coppelia was inspired
by folk music and dancing
from Hungary.

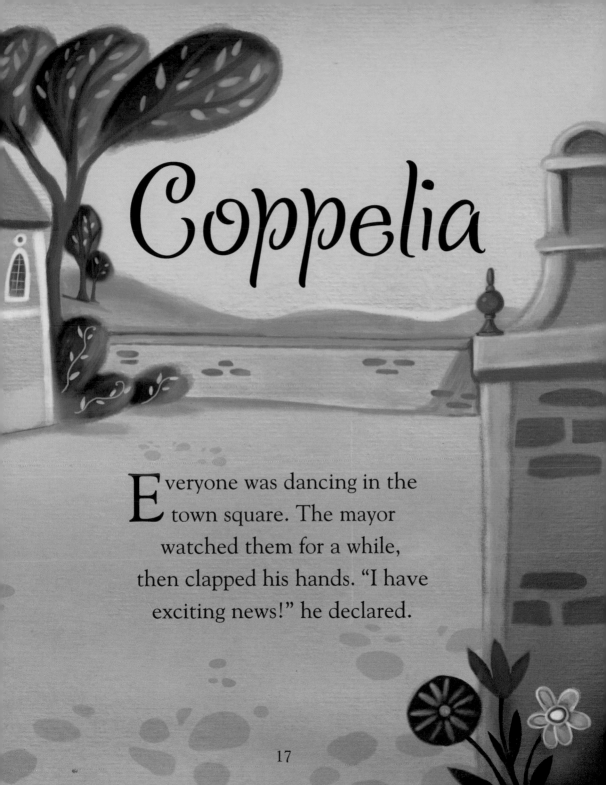

Coppelia

Everyone was dancing in the town square. The mayor watched them for a while, then clapped his hands. "I have exciting news!" he declared.

"Soon, our village will have a brand new bell. To celebrate, we will hold a festival. And what's more, all the couples who decide to get married on that day will be given a purse full of gold."

In the midst of the applause, one of the dancers turned to her sweetheart.

"That could be us, Franz," Swanhilda whispered in his ear.

"Yes, my love," said Franz, smiling dreamily. The band struck up, and they began to dance again, twirling across the town square.

"We're so lucky," said Swanhilda, as they danced. "Don't you think so, Franz?"

Franz didn't reply.

"What are you looking at?" asked Swanhilda.

"What? Nothing!" said Franz.

But Swanhilda followed his gaze to the house of the inventor, Dr. Coppelius, where a girl sat reading on a balcony.

Dr. Coppelius was a strange man, but his daughter, Coppelia, was stranger still.

"You're looking at Coppelia again!" cried Swanhilda, filled with jealousy. "What's so special about her anyway? She might be pretty, but she never moves! She never speaks! I've never even seen her leave that house. All she does all day is read, read, read."

"I have to go," Franz said suddenly.

With a quick kiss to her forehead, he hurried away from the dance. Swanhilda was left alone, surrounded by laughing couples.

As Swanhilda walked home that night, she knew she couldn't marry Franz. He said he still loved her... but she no longer believed him.

Later, she crept back to the town square. She wanted to meet Coppelia for herself. But there was Franz, standing below the balcony.

"Coppelia!" Franz called out. "Please, won't you talk to me? You know how I long to hear your voice."

He blew a kiss up to the balcony, but the girl carried on reading.

"Coppelia, stop torturing me. Just look at me," he begged.

Unseen by Franz, Swanhilda fought back her tears.

When Franz had gone, she rushed across the square, and stood under the balcony herself.

"Coppelia?" said Swanhilda. "Coppelia, please speak to me."

But the mysterious girl merely continued to read.

Swanhilda waved to her, curtseyed to her, even danced for her, but Coppelia refused to acknowledge her.

"Fine!" snapped Swanhilda. "Don't speak to me then. See if I care!"

And still the wretched girl said nothing.

"Swanhilda!" came a shout. "Come and help us." It was her friends, holding bundles of flags and decorations for the festival. Swanhilda hurried over.

As she told them what had happened, Dr. Coppelius himself came out of his house, and bustled past them.

"Out of my way!" he barked.

There was a tinkling sound. Swanhilda looked around and spotted his key, lying on the ground. A plan formed in her mind. She whispered it to her friends. "What do you think? Shall we?"

That evening, Swanhilda put his key in the lock and pushed open the door. The other girls hung back, nervous, but Swanhilda beckoned them on. Then the girls tiptoed up the stairs to the inventor's workshop...

The air smelled strange, of sawdust and spices. At the far end of the room sat Coppelia, swathed in a shawl, reading by lamplight.

"Coppelia? Coppelia?" said Swanhilda, stepping nervously into the room. "I want to talk to you about Franz."

Coppelia ignored her.

"Please," she begged, stepping even closer. Then she gasped. "She's... not real," Swanhilda spluttered. "She's – she's a doll."

"So this is Franz's perfect woman," laughed her friends, pushing Coppelia onto the floor. They set about exploring the workshop, pulling back dust sheets, peering into dark corners.

"Look!" said Swanhilda, turning a rusty key in a toy soldier. With a low, whirring sound, the soldier began to walk across the room.

They wound up more and more toys. Soon the room was alive with a strange procession of dolls.

"What do you think you're doing?"

Swanhilda turned to see Dr. Coppelius rushing towards her, his eyes blazing with rage.

"Out! Get out! All of you! NOW!"

With a flurry of feet, the girls flew from the workshop.

"Idiots! Wretches!" cried Dr. Coppelius, cradling Coppelia in his arms.

A thumping sound from the balcony made him turn. Gently, he placed Coppelia on a chair and covered her with her shawl.

"Who's there?" he called out. "Ha!" he added, as he spotted Franz, attempting to hide. "How did you get there? Don't be shy. Are you here to see Coppelia? She's often spoken of you."

"I climbed up a ladder," said Franz, blushing as he came forward. "Has Coppelia really spoken of me?"

"Oh yes," chuckled Dr. Coppelius. "And tonight you shall meet. First, let's have a drink."

The doctor poured out a glass of rich, fragrant wine.

"To young love," he said, handing Franz the

glass. He watched, smiling, as Franz drank it down. Moments later, Franz tottered and swayed, then sank into a chair, eyes closed.

"Good, good," cried the doctor. "It begins!" He clapped his hands. "Tonight, Coppelia will live! Now, where is my spellbook?"

Dr. Coppelius plucked his spellbook from the shelf, then unwrapped Coppelia and brought her into the middle of the room.

He lifted up his arms, and in a thundering voice, he commanded:

"Spirits! Take the soul of this young boy, take his spark of life. One young heart shall die and one be born. Bring Coppelia to life."

Coppelia blinked her eyes once... twice. The doctor caught his breath. Slowly, very slowly, she looked around.

Then she began to move her hands, as if she'd only just discovered them. At last slowly... gracefully... she began to dance around the workshop.

"It worked," cried Dr. Coppelius. A tear trickled down his cheek. "It worked. Franz is dead but you are alive."

Dr. Coppelius waved his arms, only for Coppelia to begin leaping and twirling across the floor.

As she danced, Franz began to rub his eyes.

Dr. Coppelius looked at Franz, and then back at the doll, flabbergasted.

"But... " said the doctor. The doll turned to him, and began to laugh.

"It's me, Swanhilda!" she said. "Couldn't you tell?" Drawing back a curtain, she showed him where she had hidden his lifeless doll.

"You witch! You tricked me!" cried Dr. Coppelius. "You're not getting away with this! You've ruined everything."

"Come on Franz, quick!" Swanhilda grabbed Franz's hand, and together they fled down the stairs, and out into the street.

"I've been such a fool," said Franz, as they turned a corner. "You rescued me."

"I saw you climbing up to the balcony and I couldn't leave you. Not in that crazy man's house. Yes, you are an utter fool," said Swanhilda, smiling. "But I love you."

The next morning, the festival began. The new bell was unveiled, and in the midst of the cheering crowds were Franz and Swanhilda, who were married that very day.

In Swan Lake, the roles of the Swan Queen, Odette, and her rival, Odile, are usually played by the same ballerina.

Swan Lake

I n a royal castle long ago, a magnificent
party was just beginning. Everyone
wanted to celebrate the prince's
twenty-first birthday.

A trumpet fanfare announced the prince's arrival.

"Happy Birthday, Your Highness!" cried the guests in unison.

The orchestra began to play and waltzing couples were soon dancing around the courtyard. Prince Siegfried looked on happily, until he saw the queen striding purposefully towards him. The musicians fell silent, the villagers froze, the courtiers bowed low.

"A birthday gift," said the queen, handing Siegfried a beautiful crossbow.

"Thank you, Mother," replied the prince.

"And now you are 21," she went on, "you must marry. The most beautiful

ladies in the kingdom will be at your birthday
ball tomorrow. You can choose one of them to
be your wife."

Without waiting for a reply, the queen
glided away. The music started up again, but all
happiness had drained from Siegfried's face.

"Cheer up," said his friends. "We can still go
hunting tonight."

Prince Siegfried loved hunting. He needed
no persuading.

Just then, a flock of swans flew overhead,
their white feathers gleaming in the moonlit sky.

"Let's follow them!" he called, leading
the way through the royal forest, his
new crossbow held high.

Siegfried tried to forget his mother's words, but they hung heavily on his mind. When the hunting group reached the shores of a lake, Siegfried urged the others to go on without him.

"I'm too young to marry," he thought, kicking a stone into the lake in frustration.

As he watched ripples spread across the water, he saw the swans land silently on the silvery surface. He slowly lifted his crossbow, took aim and... stopped in amazement.

The nearest swan was rising up out of the water. It beat its snowy wings and transformed into a beautiful woman. She wore a downy white dress and a delicate, moon-bright crown. In a few graceful steps, she was standing on the shore.

"Who *are* you?" asked Siegfried in wonder.

The woman drew back in fear.

"I won't hurt you, I promise," he said, laying down his crossbow. "I'm Prince Siegfried. What's your name?"

His kind face and gentle words gave the woman confidence. "I am Odette," she said, in a soft, musical voice, "the Queen of the Swans."

Odette beckoned to the other swans and one by one they emerged as beautiful maidens, glistening from the water. They all looked perfect, except for a sadness in their eyes.

"We are under a spell," explained Odette, "to be swans by day and our true selves only by night."

Siegfried was appalled. "Who has done this to you?" he asked.

"Von Rothbart," replied Odette, "an evil magician.

38

Each night he turns into an owl and watches over us."

"Can't the spell be broken?"

Odette slowly shook her head. "Only if someone promises to love me forever."

Siegfried's heart went out to Odette. All he wanted in the world was to protect her. He held her in his arms and they danced dreamily in the moonlight. The other swan-maidens linked arms and danced too, filled with new hope.

But von Rothbart was watching them. "I won't let that prince break my spell," he muttered.

At the first
glow of dawn, he
emerged from the
shadows and stood
wings outstretched
in front of Siegfried.
"Back to the lake!" he
ordered the swan-maidens.
"No!" cried Siegfried. "Let them go!"
But von Rothbart only sneered at him.

Odette faded from Siegfried's arms and flew
away, a swan once more. "I love you," he called
after her. "And I will set you free..."

Guests arrived from all over Europe for the
prince's birthday ball. The queen watched her
son expectantly. He danced with one glamorous
princess after another, but he looked distracted
and distant, his mind lost in thought.

After the final dance, his mother walked
over to him. "So," she said, "who have you
chosen to be your wife?"

The ballroom fell silent. All eyes were on
the prince.

"I cannot marry any of them," he said firmly.

Gasps spread around the room. The
queen turned red with rage. Then BOOM! A
thunderclap made everyone turn.

In the doorway stood two figures – a tall
man, in a midnight-blue cloak, and a beautiful
young woman in a long black dress.

"I am Duke Azio," announced the man.

"And Odette?" cried Siegfried, rushing to greet the woman. "Is that you?"

The music began again and Siegfried took her by the hand. Bewitched by her beauty, he led her in a mesmerizing dance.

He didn't notice the duke looking on triumphantly.

He didn't hear the desperate tapping at the window.

He never saw the real Odette shrink back in horror.

When the music ended, Siegfried turned to his astonished guests. "This is the woman I wish to marry," he announced proudly.

"But do you love her?" asked the duke. "Will you swear it?"

"I swear it," answered Siegfried instantly.

A cackle of laughter filled the air as the duke revealed himself to be... von Rothbart. "You have sworn your love to my daughter, Odile!" he cried. "Now you can never rescue Odette. She will be mine forever."

"No!" howled Siegfried.

In another thunderclap, the magician and his daughter were gone.

Siegfried fled the castle in despair. He raced to the lake and found the swan-maidens huddled around Odette.

"I'm so sorry," said Siegfried, throwing himself at her feet. "Von Rothbart used his magic to make his daughter look like you."

"I saw you dancing with her," said Odette.
"I wanted to warn you. Now we can never
be together."

"I'm here now," whispered Siegfried.

Then a dark shadow fell over them.

"Too late!" snarled von Rothbart, towering
up from behind. "She's *mine*."

He captured Odette under his feathery wings
and dragged her away from the prince.

"Never!" cried Siegfried, chasing after them.
He lunged at von Rothbart, but the magician
laughed and leaped to one side, sending
Siegfried sprawling to the ground.

Picking himself up he charged at the magician again. This time von Rothbart stumbled and loosened his grip on Odette. She escaped from under his wings and fled to the rocks above the lake.

When she looked back at Siegfried, her eyes were brimming with tears. "I'm sorry," she cried. "This is the only way I can be free." Raising her arms, she threw herself from the rocks.

"I'm not losing you again," cried Siegfried, clambering up the rocks and diving in after her.

As the silvery water closed over them both, von Rothbart let out a groan and slumped to the ground. Siegfried's act of pure love had broken his spell, and now all power was draining from him.

The swan-maidens stood speechless, watching the sun rise above the lake. They were free at last, but they had lost their queen.

A sudden movement caught their eye. Two swans burst out of the lake, spraying water from their wings. Side by side they soared into the morning light, never to be parted again.

La Sylphide is French for 'the sylph'
– an imaginary spirit of the air.

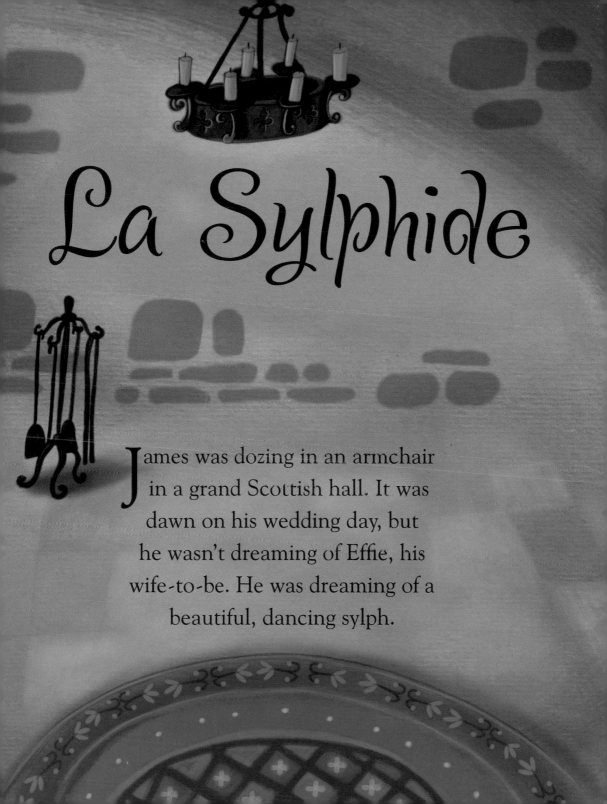

La Sylphide

James was dozing in an armchair
in a grand Scottish hall. It was
dawn on his wedding day, but
he wasn't dreaming of Effie, his
wife-to-be. He was dreaming of a
beautiful, dancing sylph.

A soft kiss on his forehead
woke him... and there she
was, as beautiful as in his
dream, spinning away
from him.

"Wait!" James cried.
"Who are you? Are you real?"

But the sylph glided to the fireplace and up
the chimney. She was gone before James could
reach her.

"Gurn!" he called out. "Did you see that?"

A sleepy figure appeared in the doorway.
"See what?" he replied, rubbing his eyes.

"Only the most stunning thing I have ever
laid eyes on," said James dreamily.

"Effie!" cried Gurn, as James' fiancée walked
in. He ran over to welcome her, but she only
had eyes for her beloved James.

"We'll be married in a few hours," she said, her cheeks pink with pleasure.

James smiled back, but couldn't help stealing a glance at the fireplace. There was no sign of the sylph now, only an old hag who had crept into the hall.

"Hey, what are you doing here?" he shouted. "Get out!"

"I'm not doing any harm," she replied. "I've just come to tell your fortunes."

"Oh yes please," piped Effie, excitedly. "I want to know how many children we're going to have."

She held out her hand and called James over to do the same.

The old hag peered down her nose at them both. "You are soon to marry..." she began.

Effie nodded eagerly.

"But not him," she added pointedly.

"That's preposterous!" blurted James, snatching back his hand.

Effie kept quiet, her eyes fixed on the hag.

"Don't worry," she went on, "you'll marry his friend instead. He's much nicer."

"Enough!" shouted James bundling the woman out of the room. "I forbid you to set foot in this house again."

"You'll be sorry..." spat the hag as she headed for the door.

James turned to Effie.

"She's completely crazy," he told her. "Today is *our* special day."

Effie nodded, desperate to believe him, but she couldn't help feeling a niggle of doubt. "Only wedding day nerves," she told herself, racing off to get ready and leaving James alone with his thoughts.

A shadow appeared at the window – surely only his imagination. Then the window opened and the sylph from his dreams floated in.

James was torn between reaching out for her and turning away from her beauty.

"I love you," the sylph said simply. "And I think you love me."

"I can't love you," James cried. "I'm marrying Effie."

"You don't have to," replied the sylph.

James watched, entranced, as she spun her magic around him, twirling, swooping, teasing.

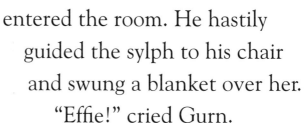

Too late, he noticed that Gurn had entered the room. He hastily guided the sylph to his chair and swung a blanket over her.

"Effie!" cried Gurn.

"Come quick. James is with another woman."

Footsteps clattered down the stairs as Effie and her bridesmaids came running. Gurn strode over to the chair and swept off the blanket to reveal... nothing.

"Oh Gurn," groaned Effie, "that's not funny."

"But..." he protested.

James breathed a sigh of relief.

The first wedding guests bustled in and soon the hall was swaying with music and dancing.

Effie beamed at James and he smiled back. Everything seemed perfect, until James spied his sylph once more. No one else even noticed her, but James saw her everywhere. She was tempting him to follow her, leave the wedding, leave behind his life...

When the bride and groom were about to exchange rings, the sylph snatched James' ring and glided out of the room. Without hesitation, James fled after her.

"James!" howled Effie in dismay.

Meanwhile, in a misty forest glade, the old hag was up to mischief. Prancing around a bubbling cauldron, she chanted:

Magic veil, do not fail.

Trick young James and ruin his games.

Carefully, she pulled a lacy white veil from the cauldron, then scurried into hiding.

Before long, the sylph arrived in the forest glade, pursued by the besotted James. He longed to hold her in his arms, but she was a spirit of the air and kept slipping from his grasp. She joined her sisters, flitting among the forest branches, while James looked on in frustration.

"Take this veil," croaked a familiar voice. "Put it on her shoulders and she will be yours..."

James eyed the old hag suspiciously, then noticed in alarm that the sylphs were disappearing. He grabbed the veil and ran.

Moments later, Effie and Gurn arrived in the glade. "How could he just run away like that?" she cried. "And on our wedding day..."

"Better than deserting you *after* the wedding," said Gurn, taking her by the hand.

"Ah, the happy couple," croaked the old hag. "I said you'd marry a nice one."

"You don't understand..." Effie began.

"Oh, don't I?" spoke the hag, her lips curling into a smile.

"She's right, Effie," said Gurn, going down on one knee. "We're meant for each other. Will you marry me?"

There was a glimmer of happiness in Effie's crestfallen face as the couple left the forest.

James knew nothing of this. He was stumbling after his beloved sylph. "Wait for me!" he yelled breathlessly. "I've found a way we can be together."

The other sylphs hovered and watched as their sister landed gracefully next to James. She stood like a statue while he draped the veil around her. Then he took her in his arms – and cried out in despair. His sylph had dissolved into the air.

At that moment, the church bells rang out for Effie and Gurn's wedding.

"Poor James," cackled the old hag. "You wanted something you couldn't have... and now you've ended up with nothing."

The starring roles in this ballet are Kitri and Basilio. The part of Don Quixote is usually taken by an older dancer.

Don Quixote

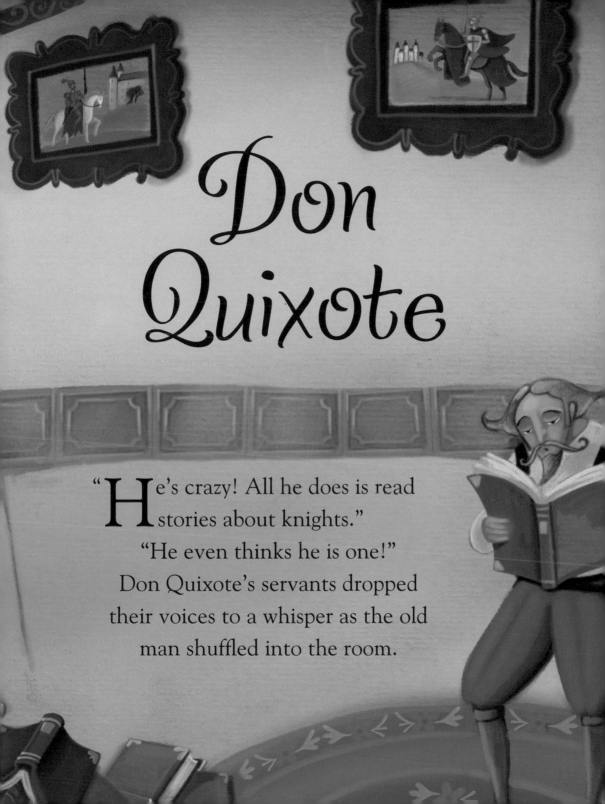

"He's crazy! All he does is read stories about knights."
"He even thinks he is one!" Don Quixote's servants dropped their voices to a whisper as the old man shuffled into the room.

He was so absorbed in his book, he didn't even notice his servants huddled in the corner. In his mind, he was jousting in a foreign field, wrestling with giants, rescuing damsels in distress. He sat down in his chair, closed his eyes and began to dream...

He was woken by the sound of shattering glass as his servant, Sancho Panza, came bursting in through the window, pursued by a horde of screaming women.

"That man stole my goose!" shrieked one.

"Away with you!" answered Don Quixote. "Your voices disturb my dreams. Out of my room. All of you!"

He shooed them away, waited until the room was quiet once more, then turned to his servant.

"Sancho Panza, I have decided to set out in search of adventure. I am a knight and it is my duty to defend the virtue of maidens, to fight dragons and giants. You are to be my squire. Now, where's my helmet..."

To Sancho Panza's surprise, Don Quixote reached for his shaving basin and plonked it on his head.

"And my lance," he went on, trying to pick up a heavy iron poker.

"Are you ready?"

"I'm ready," replied Sancho Panza, with a shrug. What else could he do but follow his crazy master?

"Aha!" said Don Quixote as they reached a town square. "This is where our adventure begins."

There was a large crowd gathered in front of an inn, cheering excitedly. A group of street dancers, dressed in flaming red cloaks, were putting on a show.

They leaped this way and that, flourishing their cloaks, enacting a dramatic bull fight.

As the dance came to an end, Don Quixote approached the innkeeper. "Greetings," he called out. "You must be the owner of this castle. And you," he added, turning to the innkeeper's beautiful daughter, "must be *Dulcinea*, the lady of my heart."

"My name is Kitri," said the innkeeper's daughter defiantly. "And my heart belongs to Basilio."

"No it does not," snapped her father. "He is nothing but a poor barber. You are to marry Gamache," he insisted, turning to the richly-dressed nobleman beside him.

Gamache bowed low to Kitri, but she dismissed him with a wave of her hand.

While the innkeeper invited Don Quixote and Gamache inside, Sancho Panza stayed in the town square, where a crowd of young people began to tease and torment him. He was spun around, tossed in the air...

"Stop that!" cried Don Quixote, rushing back outside to save his squire, the innkeeper following on behind.

"Where is my daughter?" demanded the innkeeper.

"She's gone!" said Gamache, searching the crowds. "And so has Basilio."

"Then let's find them! And then I will announce her marriage to *you*, Gamache."

"And we will go too!" whispered Don Quixote. "Come, squire. It seems Kitri's heart is already taken. Our mission is to make sure she marries her true love, Basilio."

They rode out of the town and into the hills, where large windmills stood against the sky, their sails like waving arms.

"Giants!" Don Quixote cried in excitement, pointing to the windmills. "We must attack!"

"Come back!" called Sancho Panza, but there was no stopping his master, who rushed at a windmill, wildly waving his poker.

Sancho Panza could only watch in horror as the windmill's sails swooped down and caught Don Quixote by his cloak, flinging him up, up, up into the air, then hurling him to the ground.

Sancho Panza ran to his injured master, but Don Quixote lay unconscious and nothing would wake him. He was dreaming again... In his dreams he saw Kitri, who appeared to him as Dulcinea, the lady of his heart, surrounded by tree nymphs and fairies.

He woke to find himself at the inn. Kitri and Basilio were standing over him, greeting him like an old friend.

"Sancho Panza brought you here to rest," said Kitri.

Before she could say more, her father and Gamache burst into the inn.

"There is to be no more running away!" stormed her father. "You *will* marry Gamache."

"I can't bear it!" sobbed Basilio. He took out his sword and thrust it into his chest.

With a wail, Kitri flung herself across his fallen body.

"A tragedy!" said Don Quixote. "*You*, innkeeper, should have listened to your daughter's heart."

"Give Basilio his dying wish," pleaded Kitri.

"Yes," insisted Don Quixote. "Give this young couple your blessing. Basilio is sure to die. Why not ease his last moments?"

The innkeeper looked at their earnest faces. "Fine, fine!" he snapped. "What does it matter now! You have my blessing to marry Basilio."

On those words Basilio leaped to his feet, kissing the innkeeper and shouting for joy.

"You're not hurt at all!" fumed the innkeeper. "I've been tricked."

"And we are to be married!" smiled Kitri, her hand in Basilio's. She turned to Don Quixote. "And you," she went on, "will be our most important guest."

The wedding day dawned with feasting
and merrymaking, then the guests took to
the floor in a lively dance. Don
Quixote watched it all with a
benevolent smile.
"Thank you, great
knight," called out Kitri.
"And thanks to your
faithful sword-bearer. This
dance is for you."
As Kitri and Basilio whirled
across the floor, the crowd cheered.
"Come, Sancho Panza," said Don Quixote.
"Our mission is at an end.
We have united Kitri
with her sweetheart.
It is time we
returned home."

The Nutcracker ballet is traditionally
performed each year around
Christmas time.

The Nutcracker

It was Christmas Eve, and the Stahlbaum family was preparing for a party. Clara carefully added the final decorations to the Christmas tree. "Magical!" exclaimed her mother.

Soon the room was abuzz with music and laughter. The last guest to arrive was an old man in a black cloak. The other children shrank away from him, but Clara and her brother Fritz ran forward in delight. It was their godfather, the wonderful toymaker, Herr Drosselmeyer.

"I have a surprise," he announced.

To everyone's amazement, he brought in two life-sized, clockwork dolls. As he wound them up they came jerkily to life, the pretty pink doll twirling gracefully and the brightly painted harlequin leaping and spinning.

When the dance was over, the old man beckoned to his godchildren. "And here are some presents just for you," he whispered.

Fritz unwrapped a beautiful drum without a word of thanks. He was much more interested in Clara's wooden soldier.

"It's a nutcracker," explained their godfather. "Watch this..." He placed a nut in the soldier's mouth and cracked it open with the soldier's jaws.

Clara took her nutcracker and held it close. "Thank you, Godfather," she said.

Fritz's face clouded with jealousy. "I want a turn," he said, snatching the nutcracker. He grabbed the biggest nut he could find and tried to force it into the soldier's mouth.

"No Fritz, don't!" cried Clara, but it was too late. The soldier broke in two and Fritz ran off to hide. Clara picked up the pieces, her sad eyes meeting her godfather's.

"Don't worry," he said. "I'll mend it." And, with a mysterious wave of his handkerchief, the nutcracker was as good as new.

Clara placed it gently below the tree and joined her friends in a dance.

All too soon, the evening was over. After the last guests had left and the family had gone to bed, Clara tiptoed back downstairs in her nightgown. She picked up her nutcracker, cradled him in her arms... and fell fast asleep.

She was woken by the clock striking midnight. It was eerily dark and the Christmas tree towered over her. It seemed to be growing taller and taller. Or was Clara shrinking?

A sudden SCRITCH SCRATCH made Clara jump. Huge, snarling mice scampered out of the shadows, commanded by their wicked king.

"Help!" Clara pleaded, then blinked in astonishment.

Her nutcracker was coming to life.

He shouted an order and a line of toy soldiers came marching out of a wooden chest. "Into battle!" he commanded.

A frantic clashing of swords followed.

Soon, only the nutcracker and the Mouse King were left.

"Hand over the girl," ordered the Mouse King.

"Never!" replied the nutcracker. But he was cornered with no escape.

"I must save him," thought Clara. She tugged off one of her slippers and threw it at the Mouse King. It sailed through the air and THUMP! hit him square on the head. The Mouse King slumped to the ground.

When Clara looked back at the nutcracker, he had changed. He was no longer a soldier, but a handsome prince. "You saved my life," he said. "Thank you. Now, let me take you on an adventure."

With those words, the walls of the house faded away and a snowy forest grew up around them. A flurry of snowflakes tumbled from the sky, swirling into dancing ice fairies. Clara gazed at them, spellbound...

...until the prince whisked her on into a world beyond the forest.

"Welcome to my home," he announced. "The Land of Sweets."

Clara gasped. Absolutely everything looked good enough to eat. Mountains were topped with whipped cream, marshmallow clouds floated in the sky, lollipop trees lined a jellybean path and ahead of them stood a frosted pink castle with white chocolate turrets.

As Clara and the prince approached, a beautiful lady in a glittering tutu appeared.

"Clara," said the Nutcracker Prince. "I'd like you to meet the Sugarplum Fairy."

The fairy curtseyed gracefully and Clara copied, nervously.

"What brings you here?" the fairy asked.

When she heard of their battle with the Mouse King, she clapped her hands with glee. "This calls for some dancing!" she declared, and led them into a grand hall where a long table was laden with mouthwatering treats.

The lively music of trumpets and castanets announced the first dance – a dramatic Spanish fandango. The dancers were dressed in velvety dark brown and moved as if they were swirling through chocolate.

Next, Arabian dancers in exotic silks swayed like rising steam from a coffee cup. A chorus of flutes announced a sprightly Chinese tea dance, followed by energetic high kicks from a troupe of Russian dancers.

Clara found herself smiling and clapping, then swaying in time to a pretty waltz of ballerinas dressed as flowers.

Finally, the prince took the Sugarplum Fairy by the hand and they dazzled everyone on the dance floor.

Clara didn't want the magic to end, but already the performers were lining up, bowing, curtseying and wishing her farewell.

"Thank you so much," beamed Clara.

"Our pleasure," replied the Sugarplum Fairy.

Clara turned to the prince and gave him a hug. "I don't want to leave," she murmured, closing her eyes to hold back the tears.

When she opencd them again, she was back home, curled up under the tree. The prince was simply a nutcracker cradled in her arms.

"Was it all a dream?" she whispered to her nutcracker. He just looked back and smiled.

La Fille Mal Gardée is also known as 'The Girl Who Needed Watching'. It is the oldest ballet still being performed today.

La Fille Mal Gardée

Dawn was breaking. In the farmyard outside Lise's house, the roosters crowed and the hens clucked. Lise ran outside, looking for Colas, the man she loved.

"He's not there," she sighed. As a token of her love, she left him a pink ribbon wrapped around the gatepost, then went sadly back into the house. Moments later, Colas appeared. He tied the bow to his stick and called, joyfully, for Lise to come out.

"Away with you, farmworker!" shouted Lise's mother, Simone, chasing him off. "You're not good enough for my daughter. She's going to marry Alain, who's rich, rich, rich!"

Lise looked longingly after Colas, but her mother set her to work, churning butter. As soon as Simone's back was turned, Lise ran to meet Colas. For a dreamlike time they danced together, weaving the pink ribbon between their hands, spinning as they wound and unwound the ribbon around their waists. Then, hearing Simone, Colas took flight once more.

"This butter's not churned!" cried Simone. "What have you been up to?"

"Nothing," lied Lise.

"If you've been seeing that good-for-nothing Colas boy..." Simone stopped abruptly as Alain and his father swept into the farmyard in their pony and cart. Alain, clutching his beloved umbrella, smiled simperingly at Lise.

"Come with us!" called Alain's father, "We're going to the harvest picnic."

They climbed aboard and set off to join in the harvest celebrations. "Dance with Alain," said his father, pushing him and Lise together, but Lise flitted away into Colas' arms.

"That won't do," cried Simone, breaking them apart.

"Show us your clog dance, Simone," asked Lise's friends, hoping to change her mood.

"Oh no!" protested Simone. "I haven't danced in years. I couldn't possibly."

"*Please*," begged Lise.

"Oh, well. If you insist," said Simone, tossing away her shoes and sinking her feet into her clogs. She stomped her way across the ground. *Clickety-clackety-click. Clickety-clackety-click.* Everyone cheered her on, then joined together for a dance around the maypole, rainbow ribbons fluttering in the breeze.

But the day began to darken.
Thunder rolled across the sky,
rain lashed at the maypole.
Alain was flung this way and
that as his umbrella took flight
with the wind, then tumbled to
the ground again.

Lise and Simone arrived home in
dripping dresses and with bedraggled hair. "I
have to go out," said Simone. "But I will not
allow you to see Colas again. So I'm locking the
door behind me."

Alone in the house, Lise began to dream of
life with Colas. She danced around the room,
imagining him proposing, miming holding their
children in her arms.

"Lise!" exclaimed Colas, jumping out from
his hiding place behind the chairs.

"You were watching me!" she cried.

There was a sound at the door – the key scraping in the lock. "Oh no! Mother's home. You must hide. Quick, into my bedroom."

Lise pushed Colas inside and shut the door.

"You're looking very guilty," said Simone, marching into the room. "Hmm. I can't have any more sneaking around. Come on, into your bedroom. You'll find a wedding dress there and I want you to put it on. Alain and his father are coming with the marriage contract. And then you and Alain will be married!"

"B-b-but..." protested Lise.

"No buts," snapped Simone.

"I'm going to lock you in. I don't want any more trouble. She pushed Lise in and locked the door.

"Hurrah!" said Simone as, a moment later, she heard the sound of the pony and cart.

The door swung open and Alain and his father came hurrying in. "I have the marriage contract," cried Alain's father, waving it in the air.

Simone clapped her hands together, and handed Alain the key. "Let out your bride!" she said, pointing to the bedroom door.

Alain went to open it. And there was Lise... and Colas... kissing!

"No!" cried Simone.

"You did lock us in together, Mother," Lise pointed out. "We *love* each other."

At last, Simone relented. She took the marriage contract and tore it in two.

Colas whooped with joy. He shouted the news to the farmworkers. Even Alain looked relieved and everyone celebrated together that love had won the day.

They took to the fields, dancing and rejoicing. The house was left empty and quiet. Until Alain returned... he had forgotten his beloved umbrella.

About the ballets

Ballets are stories told with music and dancing rather than words and pictures. Composers write the music and choreographers devise the dance movements.

There are three different kinds of ballets in this book: comic, romantic and classical.

Comic ballets, such as *La Fille Mal Gardée*, *Coppelia* and *Don Quixote*, tell stories in a light-hearted, amusing way. In 1885, a performance of *La Fille Mal Gardée* by Russia's Imperial Ballet even featured live chickens on stage.

Romantic ballets were influenced by ideas of mysterious spirits, the power of nature and exotic settings. These were the first ballets to give women a starring role.

The romantic ballet *La Sylphide* was specially devised for the choreographer's daughter, Marie Taglioni. She began the tradition of ballerinas wearing shorter skirts, so that audiences could admire their footwork.

The original versions of *Swan Lake*, *The Sleeping Beauty* and *The Nutcracker* are classical ballets. They require very precise techniques, including pointe work (balancing on the tips of the toes) and high leg extensions (holding one leg out high and straight), in order to make the movements more graceful.

Over time, the ballets have been adapted for new audiences, but the earlier versions are still performed today.

Usborne Quicklinks

For links to websites where you can watch video clips of dancers performing in the ballets in this book, go to the Usborne Quicklinks website at **www.usborne.com/quicklinks** and enter the keywords **'ballet stories for bedtime'**.

When using the internet, please follow the internet safety guidelines shown on the Usborne Quicklinks website. The links at Usborne Quicklinks are regularly reviewed and updated, but Usborne Publishing is not responsible and does not accept liability for the content on any website other than its own. We recommend that all children are supervised while using the internet.

Edited by Lesley Sims   Designed by Caroline Spatz

Additional design by Lucy Wain

Digital manipulation by John Russell

First published in 2013 by Usborne Publishing Ltd., Usborne House, 83-85 Saffron Hill, London EC1N 8RT, England. www.usborne.com
Copyright © 2013 Usborne Publishing Ltd.